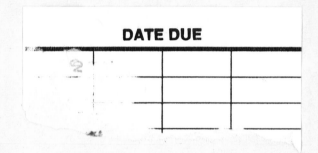

DATE DUE

Be sure to look for all the great McGee and Me! books and videos at your favorite bookstore.

Focus on the Family

PRESENTS

THE NEW ADVENTURES

McGEE

and me!

The
Blunder
Years

Bill Myers and Robert West

Based on characters created by Bill Myers and Ken C. Johnson,
the story by George Taweel and Rob Loos, and the screenplay
by Brian Bird and John Wierick.

Tyndale House Publishers, Inc.
Wheaton, Illinois

For Scott Kennedy—friend, brother, and fellow servant.

Library of Congress Cataloging-in-Publication Data

Myers, Bill, date
    The blunder years / Bill Myers and Robert West.
        p. cm.
    "Focus on the Family presents McGee and me!"
    "Based on characters created by Bill Myers and Ken C. Johnson and
the screenplay by Brian Bird and John Wierick."
    Summary: When thirteen-year-old Nicholas and his cartoon friend
McGee hook up with the coolest guy in school, Nicholas turns into a
major jerk before realizing that it is more important to be yourself.
    ISBN 0-8423-4117-X
    [1. Self-acceptance—Fiction.   2. Cartoon characters—Fiction.
3. Schools—Fiction.   4. Christian life—Fiction.]   I. West,
Robert, 1945-   .   II. Title.
PZ7.M98234B1   1993
[Fic]—dc20   93-964

Printed in the United States of America
99 98 97 96 95 94 93
 7   6   5   4   3   2

Contents

Men judge by outward appearance, but [God looks] at a man's thoughts and intentions.
(1 Samuel 16:7, *The Living Bible*)

ONE
Beginnings

It was worse than twenty-four hours of nonstop
"Brady Bunch" reruns. More terrifying than clean-
ing out the bottom of your gym locker. More disgust-
ing than lima beans in cream gravy.

Well, maybe not that bad, but close.

Nicky boy was trying something new as he
sketched in my beautiful baby blues and fantasti-
cally fabulous face. I wanted to move around and
see what he was up to, but since he hadn't drawn
my legs yet, moving anywhere was a little on the
impossible side.

"Whatcha up to, buddy boy?" I shouted.

No answer. He just kept sketching. At last he got
around to my magnificent bod—that renowned
hunk of handsomeness that causes women around
the world to swoon in ecstasy, to scream in hyste-
ria, to beg me never to take off my shirt. . . .

I craned my neck for a better look. Nicky's pencil
was moving faster than a little kid making the
rounds on Halloween. But . . . hey! Oh no! Hold the

phone . . . could it be? I couldn't believe my eyes!
Nick was trading in my perfect pudginess for something leaner, meaner, and less huggable.

He was changing me!

"What are you doin'?" I shouted. "That ain't me!"

Instead of giving me an answer, he quickly
sketched in a button-down collar.

"What?"

Then a pinkie ring the size of a Buick.

"Nick??"

Suddenly I was wearing pleated pants.

"NICHOLAS!!"

And saddle shoes.

"AUGH!"

Then . . . horror of horrors, worst of worsts, catastrophe of catastrophes! No, we aren't talkin' world
hunger or thermonuclear war. We aren't even talkin'
collapse of the universe. It was worse. Much worse.

We're talkin' about changing my hair!!!

"No, Nicholas! Not the—"

I was too late. Suddenly my golden locks were replaced with an Elvis Presley hairdo. Then, before I
could croon out a quick "You ain't nothin' but a
hound dog," Nick's pencils started scratching and
filling the rest of me in with loud, obnoxious colors.

"Cut it out, kid, that tickles!"

He didn't cut it out. He just kept going until he
was done. I looked down at his work . . . AU-
UGGHHH!

"What's going on?" I screamed. "I look like a
game show host!"

"Lighten up, McGee," Nick scolded. "We're in ju-

junior high now. We gotta get a new look. Make a statement. Be hip."

"Hip-schmip!" I cried as I tried to slip out of my clothes and adjust my oversized, hairspray-stiff hair. "Change me back!"

"OK." Nick shrugged as he picked up his eraser. In a minute he'd fixed my hair and had me back into my red, white, and blues . . . complete with standard issue suspenders and sneakers.

With a sigh of relief, I hopped off the pad and demanded, "What's gotten into you, anyway?"

"Whaddya talking about?" Nick said. But he wasn't looking at me—he was too busy looking in the mirror and giving his hair a quick work over.

I frowned. Something was up. I strolled over to the edge of the drawing table. "Ever since you started hanging around with that Rex guy at school, you've been acting different!" I insisted.

Nick gave his comb a flick. "That's because Rex Rogers, who happens to be the coolest guy at Eastfield Junior High, is gonna show me what's cool." He dropped his comb into his pocket like a gunfighter holstering his pistol. "In fact, he's coming over in a few."

"A few what?" I asked.

"A few, you know, minutes."

The kid was in worse shape than I thought. If he kept this up his ego was gonna be bigger than mine. And this house wasn't big enough for that—come to think of it, neither was the universe. I glanced down at my feet. "Augghh! You drew my shoes on backwards." The boy blunder didn't even notice, so I sat down and tried to change them

11

myself. "If you ask me—" I gave my right shoe a tug—"Ughhh! Old Rexy's a little too—uuuuumph!—cool for his own—grrrrr!—good." I finally yanked my shoe off. The only problem was when it went flying, so did I.

"AIEEEEEEEEEEEEEEE!"

Right into the wastebasket.

I tried to stay cool—though it's a little hard to be cool when you're standing inside a wastepaper basket covered in pencil shavings, with a Gooey-Chewy Bar wrapper stuck to your rear.

Nick peered over the edge and did his best not to laugh. "All I know," he said, "is if you wanna be someone in junior high, you gotta be like Rex Rogers."

Right on cue, the door flew open. Nick spun around, accidentally kicking over my trash can and sending me rolling.

"Whoaa!"

Rumble, rumble . . .

"NICHOLAS!"

Rattle, rattle . . .

"N I C H O L A S !!!"

. . . roll, roll, roll . . .

He didn't hear my yelling. As I staggered out of the wastebasket, I could see the reason why: Rex Rogers had entered the room. The Rex Rogers . . . the coolest guy this side of a Bugle Boy commercial.

There he stood . . . black jeans, black jacket (com plete with pushed-up sleeves), all wrapped around a plain white shirt and socks. And let's not forget those Ray·Ban®s. Day or night Rexy boy couldn't be seen without his shades. Rumor had it he even wore them in the shower.

"Hey, dude, how's it blowdryin'?" Rex quipped to his awestruck apprentice.

"Hey, Rexster." Nick fumbled for the words. "Uh . . . stylin' . . . big-time."

I thought I was going to get sick. Since when did Nick start speaking "cool-ese"?

"Cool," Rex answered as he turned to check out the room.

"Cool." Nick nodded.

(I tell you, if things got any cooler here we'd start storing sides of beef.)

Rex eyed the world-famous inventions that Nick had hanging around his room. Now it's true, a few of those inventions still needed a little work . . . like his jet-powered roller skates (which he couldn't slow down to under 200 miles per hour). Then, of course, there was his solar-powered umbrella (which could only be used on sunny days). And let's not forget his remote-controlled salad spinner. (Hey, it almost worked—'til it confused Dad's green tie for a cucumber.)

I waited for Rex's words of admiration, but instead of praising Nick on all this keen stuff, Mr. Cool just rolled his eyes and gave Nick's remote-controlled dinosaur a kick. "What's with all the kid junk?" Rexy boy complained. "Place looks like Mister Rogers' Neighborhood."

Rex turned toward my drawing table, and Nicholas quickly tossed some of his stuff under his bed. Rexy baby started admiring some of Nick's sketches of me. Well, at least the guy had taste. . . .

13

Until he opened his mouth.

"Doodles?" he asked, turning back to Nick. "Drawing doodles is very uncool."

DOODLES?! Why, if I was another five feet taller and 180 pounds heavier, I'd show this bozo a thing or two!

Suddenly Rexy spied Nick's open Bible. Nicholas squirmed nervously as Mr. Too Cool crossed over and picked it up to read: "'Men judge by the outward appearance . . . '" He looked up.

Nick waited for the verdict.

"Cool," Rex finally said. "Very, very cool."

Nicholas heaved a sigh of relief as Rex plopped the book back on the desk and continued his tour of the room.

Hold the phone! How could the Bible say anything this Popsicle could agree with?! I crawled up the chair and onto the desk to take a read for myself. I scanned down the page until I spotted it. Let's see . . . here it is: "Men judge by the outward appearance, but—"

Ahhh-haaa! A "BUT." I knew it!

I continued reading: "But God looks at a man's thoughts and intentions."

Just as I thought. That slicked-down, shady-eyed rooster missed the whole point! I looked up, ready to point this out to Nick, but he wasn't even looking my way. His eyes were glued to Rex, who was continuing his search-and-scorn mission around the room. He'd just discovered one of Nick's model planes and was holding it up like a dirty diaper, giving Nick his famous "Meltdown Look."

Nick grabbed a box. "Oh . . . ahh . . . I was just

. . . just packing up all this old stuff," he stammered as he threw everything he could grab into the box. "For the . . . the dump, you know."

Suddenly, Jamie, Nick's nine-year-old sister, burst through the door. (Jamie was great at bursting.) "Your Junior Rangers magazine came in the mail," she said, holding it out to him. "I hope you don't mind—I already cut out the recipe for raccoon cookies."

In a flash Nick snatched the magazine from her hand and stuffed it into the "junk" box. Then, before she could complain, he spun her around. "I hate to see you rush out," he said, hustling her toward the door, "but I think it's time for your four o'clock feeding."

"What? But—" she protested. With a slam, she was gone, except for some muffled complaints on the other side of the door. (She was also great at complaining.)

"Little sisters," Nick said with a shrug. "Major drag."

"Yeah." Rex nodded. "Totally juvenile."

There was an awkward moment as Nick tried to think of something else cool to say about his sister. Unfortunately, his folks had brought him up too well to say anything really mean.

"Well, uh . . . I guess we oughta study for that U.S. history test?" he finally suggested.

"Bag the books, dude," Rex replied. "What's to study about U.S. history? Christopher Columbus checked the place out. Now we're here."

"Oh yeah . . . right. Well . . . I guess we could . . ."

Nick was stumped. I mean, what do cool guys do? Then he had it!

"We could comb our hair!"

"Excellent!" Rex exclaimed. "Yer catchin' on, dude!"

They pulled out their combs and strutted to the mirror.

"Nick! Rex! Dinner!" It was Mom.

Too bad. They were just getting into the real spirit of coolness. With heavy sighs they holstered their combs and headed for the door. Rexy-Poo hesitated for one last look in the mirror, but he saw nothing to fix. (If he'd asked me, I could have given him a twenty-page list . . . single spaced . . . with lots of footnotes.)

He swiveled around and joined Nick. They headed out the door without so much as a "Catch ya later, dude" to yours truly.

I hopped into my sketch pad and strolled over to my kitchen. Needless to say, I was pretty upset about everything and figured it was time to have a good think. And what's a good think without half a dozen bags of Chee•tos, twelve Hostess Ho-Hos, and four diet Cokes? (I like to nibble when I noodle.) The best I figured, ol' Nicky boy was in for another lesson of life.

Too bad. I just hoped it wouldn't be too painful. And, of course, that he'd leave my hair alone. . . .

TWO
Losers, Weepers

While Nick and Rex were making swirlies in their hair, Mom and Jamie were downstairs putting supper on the table. Actually, Mom was "putting," Jamie was "tossing."

When Mom told her little girl to set the table, she didn't mean for Jamie to deal out the plates. But the little nine-year-old had those plates skidding across the table into place faster than Las Vegas's best dealers. Just then, Sarah flung open the door and charged into the room with her tennis racket.

"Sarah!" Jamie cried, as she ran around the table to her. "Did you ask the other players?"

"Jamie," Sarah sighed, as she flung her racket onto the couch. "You cannot be our tennis team mascot." Jamie gave a frustrated huff and returned to the table, where she started dealing out the knives and forks.

Sarah slumped into a nearby chair. "Anyway, why would you wanna be a mascot for a team that has exactly zero wins this century?" She propped her chin dejectedly on her elbow.

"Lost again?" Mom asked sympathetically.

"I'll say. I don't know why they use the word *love* when you don't score any points. It's more like total humiliation."

It was about this time that Nick and Rex ambled into the room. "Hey, Mom," Nick drawled in his coolest of cool voices. "We're ready to do dinner."

Mom hesitated a moment. "Good, 'cause I'm almost finished 'doing' salad."

Nick and Rex traded "Get real!" looks. What was an uncool grown-up doing trying to sound like a cool kid? They shrugged and sauntered over to the table. It took one millionth of a second for Rex to focus on Nick's gorgeous big sister.

"So, Sarah," he said as they all took their seats, "it's gonna be, like, only eighteen months before I hit the freshman class. Maybe you and me could get together sometime and make some memories."

Sarah looked at him like he had just dropped in from Pluto. "Sure, Rex," she quipped, wearing her best painted-on smile. "Should I pick you up at your house? Or would you rather have your mommy drop you off here?"

It was one of her better put-downs, but since "super-cool" doesn't necessarily mean "super-intelligent," Rex popped up his thumb and grinned. "Excellent!" he said.

"OK," Mom broke in, trying her best to save Rex any more humiliation. "Here we go!" She set a platter full of barbecued chicken and a basket of biscuits in front of them.

18

"B-B-Q Yard Bird?!" Rex announced enthusiastically. "I'm stoked!"

"Huh?" Mom and Jamie asked simultaneously.

Nick interpreted with a shrug. "He's excited about the chicken."

Suddenly Dad entered through the kitchen door, briefcase in hand. "Hi, everybody!"

A chorus of hellos greeted him. Even Sarah picked up her chin long enough for a halfhearted "Hi." Mom, of course, gave him a welcome-home kiss as he crossed to take his place at the table.

"Sorry I'm late," he said as he joined them. "I got a late call at the paper, but it was worth it." Wearing a mysterious grin, he paused to tuck in his napkin. Then, looking over the food, he continued, "Ahh . . . nothing like a great meal to celebrate a little great news." He paused again, waiting for a reaction.

"Great news?" Mom asked.

Dad just grinned. He had the "pregnant pause" perfected to a fine art. He'd learned to say just enough to get your ears pricked, then hold off while you sat there, curiosity building second by second until you felt like a boiler about to explode.

"Great news?" Sarah repeated hopefully. She could use a little great news. "What is it, Dad?"

"Patience." He grinned. "First, let's give thanks."

Normally, the Martins are pretty good at praying. They have no problem remembering to thank God for all his love and goodness to them. But when you're busy thinking about "great news" it can be a little hard getting your head bowed and your mind on praying.

19

For Nick, the problem was doubly bad. After all, here he was with the coolest guy in school at his table, and suddenly he's supposed to bow his head and hold hands? He wasn't sure about praying, but he knew hand holding with family members was definitely *not* in the "Handbook of Coolness."

Rex didn't have a clue what was going on until little Jamie grabbed his hand. He hesitated, but she was pretty persistent. Then, noticing everyone had bowed their heads, he lowered his.

Dad cleared his voice and began. "For this meal and those who prepared it, we thank you, Lord. Bless our home, and our friend Rex. Amen."

Quick as a flash, Nick dropped the hands he held and flashed a nervous shrug to Rex.

"So, David . . ." Mom pressed.

"Yes?" Dad asked as he buttered his biscuit.

"The news?" Mom persisted.

"What news is that?" Dad teased.

"David!"

"Dad!"

He chuckled lightly, then continued. "Well . . . Nick's principal, Mrs. Pryce, called . . . about next week's Twenty-Fifth Annual Battle of the Bands."

"You mean Endless Summer?" Nick interrupted excitedly, forgetting that cool guys don't get excited. "It's supposed to be the most awesome Battle the school's ever had." Suddenly a disturbing thought crossed his mind. "Tell me you're not chaperons!"

"Even better!" Dad grinned. "You see, twenty-five years ago, when your mom and I were eighth grad-

ers at Eastfield, the first Battle of the Bands was
. . . well . . . our idea."

"Prehistoric, dude," Rex whispered to Nick.

"Well," Dad went on, "the good news is that they've
asked us to come back and host this year's Battle."

Mom came unglued. She shrieked with delight
and practically knocked Dad off his chair with her
hug.

The other reactions in the room were somewhat
mixed.

Sarah congratulated them (grateful that they
were hosting an event for the junior high and not
the senior high). Jamie was confused just trying to
come to grips with the idea that Mom and Dad
had ever been in the eighth grade.

And Nick? Well, he looked like he had just swallowed last year's cafeteria special—"hashloaf sur-
prise"—definitely green around the gills. "You're
ho . . . ho . . . hosting?" he choked.

"That's right." Dad beamed. "This year's Battle of
the Bands is going to be a Martin family affair!"

"Oh, Nick," Mom giggled, "aren't you just . . .
just . . ." She tried desperately to think of a word
her son could relate to. A word that would help
him share her excitement: "Aren't you just
stoked?!"

Nick stared at her, his face green, his mouth
ajar. Well, so much for sharing.

Rex leaned over to him and murmured, "This is
starting to sound more like endless bummer."

"Endless bummer" was exactly what Sarah's life
on the tennis court had become.

Three days later she was again dancing from foot to foot, waiting for the final, match-point serve. It came.

She returned it beautifully.

The opposition fired it back across at Tina, Sarah's best friend and doubles partner. She fended it off perfectly.

So far, so good.

The fuzzy little ball kept whizzing back and forth until the other team slammed an across-the-court smash. Sarah dove for it and missed. *"Aaaah!"* she cried as she slid painfully into a three-point landing—leaving skid marks from her knees and elbow.

Of course, if this were a movie, she'd have clobbered the ball, come back from behind, and leapt over the net in victory. Unfortunately, it wasn't a movie. Instead it was "40-Love," "Game," "Match," and another major defeat for her team.

Slowly she got to her feet, snatched her towel, and marched toward the locker room in frustration. Tina was right behind her.

"Why didn't you let it go?" Tina snapped.

"What?"

"The ball—it was going out-of-bounds! Why didn't you let it go?"

"Because I thought it was in!" Sarah shot back. "My head was, like, four inches off the ground. Things aren't so clear with your nose that close to concrete," she growled. "Besides, if you hadn't given them a lob to smash back, I wouldn't have been in that position in the first place!"

"Gee, you know," Tina said, struggling to keep

her cool, "I really thought we could take these guys."

"Well, we couldn't." Sarah's terse answer was delivered through clenched teeth. "But it would have helped if you had stayed close to the net like you were supposed to!" With that, she sped up and burst through the locker-room door.

Usually there's nothing like a warm shower and a little locker-room chatter to cool things down. After all, Sarah was not only pretty, she was nice. The "Golden Rule" had been imprinted in her brain circuitry seventeen layers deep. Given time, it always went into effect. Well, almost always. . . .

"I never lose when I play by myself!" Sarah complained as she laced up her shoes. (Obviously the Golden Rule circuitry had shorted out somewhere.)

"And what's that supposed to mean?" Tina snapped as she whirled around to face her.

"All right, girls, that's enough!" the coach yelled from across the locker room. "Practice tomorrow at three o'clock sharp. We've got some work to do."

Neither Sarah nor Tina bothered to tune in to the announcement. Their eyes were still shooting sparks at each other.

"Are you saying you think you're better than me?!" Tina glared.

"No—I mean—" Sarah stammered, beginning to remember her Golden Rule programming. Already she had started to regret her words. "Ohhh . . . forget it. Look . . . I'm sorry. It's just that . . . that . . ."

"That what?" Tina demanded.

"I just don't like . . . losing. Especially when it's all the time."

Tina heaved a sigh. "Well, who does?"

"Come on," Sarah said, slamming her locker door closed. "Let's get out of here and face the music."

"What music is that?" Tina asked while grabbing her duffel bag.

"The music everyone's making about us losing." Sarah sighed. "It's becoming the number-one hit of the school."

THREE
Cool Guys Wear Black

Once again Nick and Rex were back in the Martins' house, and they were redefining the fashion world. To be more exact, Rex was redefining Nick's wardrobe. After all, when it comes to cool dudedom, clothes don't make the man—they *are* the man.

"What about one of these?" Nick asked as he brought a fistful of shirts out of his closet.

"Dude," Rex pronounced, examining the stack from his kicked-back position on the bed, "you gotta stop shopping at Geeks-R-Us. There's not one designer label in here."

Nick tossed the shirts across the bed and plunged back into the closet searching for more.

"Look," Rex explained, "it's like this: life is one big amusement park. All the cool people are inside, having a cool time. And all the uncool people are on the outside, trying to get tickets. Take a guess where you get tickets . . . ?"

Nick's head poked out of the closet. "I . . . I don't know."

"Junior high, dude." Rex rose from the bed and swaggered over to the mirror. "It's where the future begins, where you either get your ticket, like me—" He glided the comb smoothly through his hair. "Or . . ."

"You're left out?" Nick finished for him with a gulp. He looked at his latest handful of shirts and threw them disgustedly on top of the others.

"Exactly," Rex agreed. "But don't worry. I'm here to save you from terminal geekdom." Rex turned and glanced at the pile of shirts. "We may need to go malling."

"Huh?"

"Go to the mall," Rex translated. He circled around Nick, giving him the once-over. *"Hmmm.* Something's still missing," he mused, rubbing his chin. "I got it . . ." He pulled out a pair of shades and ceremoniously handed them to Nick. "They're yours, bro."

Nick couldn't believe his eyes. The "Rexster" was giving him his only pair of sunglasses? Incredible! Fantastic! Incredibly fantastic!

Well, not exactly . . .

Rex grinned as he drew out another pair of sunglasses and put them on. "I always keep a spare." The Ray·Ban® duo turned together, like Siamese twins, and stared admiringly into the mirror.

"Whoa . . . definitely . . . non-geeky," Nick oozed.

"Totally cool," Rex echoed.

The next day a new dude invaded Eastfield Junior High. He was . . .
THE NICKSTER.

Totally malled, totally made over, totally hip—from his black T-shirt, to his black pants, to his black shoes—Nick looked a lot like a shadow wearing sunglasses. He strutted down the hallway as cool as an ice cube on a subzero day in the Arctic.

Philip did a double take when Mr. Ray•Ban®s drifted by. *Who was that masked man?* he wondered. Then, recognizing his old pal beneath the black wrappers, he started up the staircase after him. "Hey, Nick!" he shouted. "Nick, wait up!"

"Oh . . . hi," Nicholas mumbled as Philip finally caught up with him. Mr. Cool glanced about nervously, hoping nobody was watching. Oh, sure, Philip was a friend, but he was also a geek. And, as a recent refugee from geekdom, Nick could not afford to be seen hanging around with him.

"You want to go to the computer show on Saturday?" Philip asked in eager anticipation. "I heard they've got this really cool antivirus that uncrashes your hard drive and leaves a big happy face on your screen!"

"Uh . . . I don't know." Nick shrugged, wishing Philip would disappear before they reached the top of the stairs. "I'm not really into computers anymore." Actually, he still liked the little electronic wonders, but Rex had said they weren't cool, so, of course, they were out.

"You're not interested?" Philip asked, his expression starting to fall. Nick glanced away and said nothing. "Well, OK." Philip tried to shrug it off, but it was pretty obvious that Nick's rejection hurt the little guy.

Mr. Cool One pretended not to notice. Instead he

mumbled a "Catch you later, dude" and started down the hall.

"'Dude'?" Philip coughed slightly on the word. He watched Nick saunter away, more than a little puzzled.

As Nick approached his locker he let out a sigh of relief. Ever since Rex had helped transform him to "cool," he'd been dreading the encounter with Philip, the All-School Loser. Now that it was over, Nicholas thought he'd handled it pretty well. Smooth and easy. No contamination.

Contamination! Nick paused and frowned slightly. He didn't exactly mean that Philip was some sort of impurity. Or did he?

Suddenly Rex appeared, dead ahead, surrounded by a couple of his clones and clonettes as they all headed down the hallway. Nick nodded to them and noticed somebody dangling from Rex's arm. This was not just any somebody. This somebody really had *some body*. She was the foxiest sample of femininity this side of sweet sixteen. Translation: She was hot. Or was it "cool"? (Nick hadn't entirely mastered the subtleties of "cool-ese" yet.)

"Lookin' buff, dude!" Rex said to Nick with an easy high five as they arrived. He tilted down his glasses to give Nick's outfit the once-over. "Nice kicks!"

"Thanks, dude," Nick returned proudly. He glanced shyly at the girl. "They're real leather!"

"What other kind is there?" Rex chuckled over his own wit before turning to his classy compan-

28

ion. "Babs Jenkins," he said, "meet my newest, uh
. . . friend, Nick Martin."

Friend? He called me . . . friend! Nick thought.
He felt like he'd been knighted or something.

"Do I, like, know you?" Babs asked in her best
Madonna wanna-be voice.

"Actually," Nick croaked, "I sit near you in Span-
ish."

"Oh . . . like, wow, I hadn't noticed." She lowered
her shades for a better look. "Bummer." Exactly
who or what she meant by "bummer" was hard to
tell, but it didn't matter to Nicholas—he was still
blushing under her baby blues.

Just down the hall, near his own locker, Philip
watched this little soap opera in amazement. Suddenly Renee appeared. "Hi, Philip!" she said as she
opened her locker door. Philip said nothing; he
was too busy staring. Puzzled by his silence, she
turned to follow his eyes to Rex, Babs, and—Nicholas?

"Why's Nick hanging out with Ken and Barbie?"
she quipped.

"Got me," Philip muttered.

"And when did he start dressing all in black? He
looks like Batman."

Just then, who should appear beside them but
the primo cool dude of them all—Derrick Cryder.
He slung open his locker and shoved in a load of
books.

Books? Derrick Cryder?? If this had been last
year, Philip and Renee would have passed out in
amazement. But the former bully and all-around
bad dude had undergone some heavy-duty spiri-

tual renovation last Christmas. Nobody was exactly sure what had happened, but one thing had become clear: Derrick was no longer the Derrick Cryder they all had known and hated. Not since he and Nick had had their little Christmas Eve encounter . . . and got to talking about Jesus.

"Hey," he grunted to Renee and Philip. "What's with Martin?"

"That's what we'd like to know," Philip answered absently. Suddenly he noticed who he was talking to. "Ahhh, oh, hi, Derrick." He knew Derrick had gone through some changes, but Philip didn't like to take chances. He still treated him with the utmost respect. After all, at one time, Philip had served as Derrick's personal punching bag.

Derrick didn't respond. He'd already seen enough. Without a word he slammed his locker and moved down the hall.

Meanwhile, back in Coolville, Nicholas and Rex also thought it was time to split. "So, Nick," Rex said with a glance back toward Philip and Renee, "you're going to bag that nimrod squad you usually hang out with and go to the Battle of the Bands with us, right?"

"Really?" Nick asked in astonishment. "Well, yeah . . . sure!"

"Hard to believe, huh?" Rex flashed him a grin. "Not too many kids can say they hang out with me." Then with a thumbs-up and chuckle he said, "Later, dude," and slinked on down the hall.

"Yeah . . . later." Nick gave a wave in the air, then quickly tucked his hands into his pockets. Cool dudes don't wave.

The bell rang and everyone scurried off in different directions. Everyone but Derrick. He had seen the rest of the "Too Cool to Be Real" show from down the hall. And he didn't much like the opening act.

FOUR
Who's a Wanna-be?

Sarah was supposed to be working on her chemistry experiment, but the school paper was opened next to her Bunsen burner. And right there, smack in the center page, was the headline: "Girl's Tennis Tromped . . . *Again!*"

"Why can't they just keep quiet about it?" Sarah fumed. Then she spotted it: her photograph. It was from their last match, the one where she'd lunged for the ball and skidded across the asphalt. The picture caught her flying through the air, her legs twisted awkwardly, her arms flailing. It was a great picture, if you happened to be a Raggedy Ann doll tumbling out of control. But if you were a teenager of the female persuasion and worried about what others thought, it was time for some major embarrassment. It wasn't that Sarah was mortified, it's just that she knew plastic surgery was the only way to avoid total humiliation.

"All right . . ." Her chemistry teacher's voice startled her. "What kind of reaction did you get when you added the potassium chlorate to the substance in the flask?"

Sarah scrambled to catch up. She scooted the school paper aside and fumbled through the chemical jars. In front of her were two filled flasks and a small cup holding something powdery. She rubbed her forehead trying to think. She knew that the powder was the potassium stuff, but . . .

Oh, help! she thought. *Which flask am I supposed to pour it into?*

She had two options: she could "Eeny, Meeny, Miny, Mo" between the two flasks or she could admit she wasn't listening and ask for help. But since she'd just seen her photo and wasn't in the mood for any more humiliation, she gave a heavy sigh and "Eeny, Meeny, Miny, Moed" it. She picked up the potassium and poured it into the "Mo" flask.

Suddenly it became clear that "Miny" would have been the better move. There was a bright flash accompanied by a small, but very impressive *KA-BOOOOOOOOOOOM!!*

"*Aughhh!*" Sarah screamed, leaping backward off her stool. She crashed into the student behind her, causing him to sprawl into his own experiment, sending his flasks and beakers crashing to the ground.

It wasn't exactly a nuclear meltdown, but it was close enough. There was something about the way the fireball in Sarah's flask kept burning and the nearby students kept running and screaming that kind of got everyone's attention.

"What's going on there?" the teacher shouted. "*Sarah!?*"

He raced to her side and swept the fireball flask into the sink, then turned on the water full blast. Finally, when the fire was out, he turned to Sarah. His look could have burned through steel.

Sarah was not intimidated. Her response was clear and to the point: "Uh . . . I . . . that is to say . . . uh . . ."

Several minutes later, Sarah was on her hands and knees wiping up the floor. All the other students had gone to lunch. Her teacher loomed above her like a thundercloud. A very angry thundercloud.

Finally she rose to her feet, looking more than a little sorrowful. "Mr. Murchison, I'm so sorry. I—I—"

"We'll talk about it Monday," he said as he headed for the door. "If you don't mind, I'll try to enjoy the last twenty minutes of my lunch break. Just hang up the rags in the cabinet and pull the door shut when you leave." With that he was gone.

Sarah pulled the rubber gloves up higher on her arms as she dropped back to her knees to resume wiping up the spill. *What a day,* she thought. *First my picture in the paper, then this mess . . . what else could go wrong?*

"Hi, Sarah."

She looked up, startled. For a moment, the sweat in her eyes fogged her vision. She blinked. Morgan Jefferson! It couldn't be! She blinked again . . . and he was still there. No big deal, of course, except that he just happened to be Eastfield High's star quarterback and number-one Junior Class Heartthrob!

She quickly sat up, wiping her face with her

34

sleeve. What lousy timing! Here she was with this awesome hunk of teenage maledom and what was she doing? Playing Cinderella . . . and without the glass slipper!

"Oh, hi," she said, trying somehow to look a little dignified.

"I felt kind of bad, leaving you here all alone," he said. "After all, some of the mess was mine."

"Yours?" Sarah asked, startled.

"Well, yeah. If you remember, I was the guy behind you when the fireworks started."

"That was you I bumped into?" Suddenly Sarah felt even more embarrassed. "It wasn't your fault," she stammered. "I was the klutz who made you knock all your stuff over."

"True," he laughed. "If it had been football, you'd have been called for clipping." He knelt down beside her and took one of her rags. "But I'm from the old school that says a guy never lets a girl take the rap by herself."

"Well . . . thanks," she said, barely able to find her voice. She couldn't believe it. Here he was, Morgan Jefferson, All-School Everything, scrubbing right alongside her.

"Don't tell my mom I did this," he said with a grin. "The next thing you know, she'll be having me scrub the kitchen floor on a regular basis."

"I promise." Sarah laughed. Then after a moment she said, "Now all I have to do is find some way to salvage my chemistry grade."

"You?" Morgan asked with a chuckle. "The class brain?"

"What do you mean 'class brain'?" she shot

back, smiling. "You're the one who's always got the answers."

"Just luck," he said with a shrug, "and the fact that I always look over your shoulder to get them." He laughed as she gave him an astonished, wide-eyed look.

Sarah had always felt shy around Morgan. Eastfield High's football team was the best they'd been in years, and everybody said it was because of him. Then there was the little matter of him being the best-looking and nicest boy in school. Some of the girls had told Sarah they'd seen him looking at her, but she knew better. Or at least, she thought she did. After all, Morgan could have his pick of any girl in Eastfield . . . or of the whole state, for that matter.

Yet, here they were. What had started out so wrong was suddenly starting to look like something so right. It *was* Cinderella time, and she didn't even need the glass slipper.

"What's this?" Morgan asked, flipping over Sarah's waterlogged school paper, which happened to be on the floor beside him. "So what's in the news today? Ah yes, the tennis team."

Sarah winced. If he read any further, he'd see her name. If he looked at the picture he'd recognize her face. She had to do something fast. Quickly she rose from the floor and began picking up all the trash. "We'd better hurry or we'll completely miss lunch," she said as she tried to snatch the paper from his hands.

No luck. Morgan hung on.

"Zero and seven!" He whistled as he continued

to scan the article. "What a bunch of losers. They just can't get it together, can they?"

Sarah looked frantically about. "Uh, I . . . I'm sure th-they're doing the best they—" Then she saw it: a small beaker of water on the workbench just above Morgan and the paper. She swallowed hard—she had no other choice. She reached over to the beaker and deliberately knocked it off the workbench.

"Hey!" Morgan yelled as the water spilled across the article and Sarah's picture.

"Sorry," she said as she snatched the soggy paper from his hands. "This just doesn't seem to be my day." She gave a silent sigh of relief as she crossed over and dumped the wadded-up paper into the trash. Of course, she couldn't keep this up forever. Somebody was bound to become suspicious if she kept running around ripping papers out of everybody's hands. For now, though, it was the only plan she had.

Morgan picked up their rags and hung them on the rack in the cabinet. "Man, I hate to lose," he said, not giving up the subject.

"Me, too," Sarah agreed softly. She took off her gloves and laid them on the counter, but before she could pick up her books Morgan scooped them into his hands and nodded toward the door.

"After you."

"Thanks." Sarah walked ahead of him, beaming like a searchlight as they headed into the hall.

"I tell you," he continued, "if our football team was doing that badly I couldn't even show my face in the school."

Sarah swallowed hard. She looked down, praying none of the passing students would notice her while they headed down the hall.

Back in junior-high land, Nick was showing his face everywhere. Only it was his new-and-not-so-improved face. The last class of the day was over when he ran into Renee near his locker.

"So, what's with the new look?" Renee asked as she approached.

Since cool guys don't study, Nick tossed his books into his locker. "What's wrong?" he shot back. "Too cool for you?"

"No . . ." His attitude caught Renee a little off guard. "It's fine. It's just . . . different."

"Well, I wouldn't expect *you* to like it."

"Sooooorryyy!" Renee flung back at him angrily. Then, without another word, she stomped over to her own locker. If he wanted to be a jerk, let him be a jerk—but he'd have to do it with somebody else.

Nicholas knew his reaction might have been a little overkill, but he was only trying to better himself, to be somebody. What was wrong with that? Hey! You've got to make some sacrifices if you want to succeed.

At that moment, Jordan, the new friend on the block, took a running slide up to his locker, which was between Nick's and Renee's. Besides being a super jock (complete with letter jacket and the accompanying biceps), Jordan was a pretty good artist.

"Yo, Nick. Yo, Renee." He tossed a football in the air before trying to remember his combination.

38

Still burning, Renee gave him a halfhearted nod as she threw open her locker with a loud bang.

Nick didn't even give him that much of a greeting.

Having no idea he had just stepped into the middle of World War III, Jordan continued, "Hey Nick, ever since you showed me that 3-D thing, my drawings are really popping!"

Nick said nothing so Jordan rattled on. "Fact is, I'm thinkin' about havin' a double career: NFL quarterback and computer graphics genius!"

"That's cool," Nick said, in his best ho-hum manner.

Still clueless about the war, Jordan turned to Renee. "Hey, Renee, you guys talked about the Battle of the Bands yet? We all gonna go together or what?"

Renee brightened at the thought. "Sounds great to me." Then she added warily, "But you better check with Mr. Cool there."

Jordan turned to Nick. "How 'bout it, Nicholas?"

"Uh . . ." Nick seemed at a loss for words. It was major decision time. If he was going to make a move away from these losers, it was now or never. Finally he mumbled. "No, uh, no thanks."

Renee tried her best to hide the hurt crossing her face, but she didn't do too well. That was OK, though, since Nick wouldn't have noticed anyway. He was staring at Rex and Babs, who were making a grand entrance down the stairs. With them was a new member of the herd. She was a beauty straight out of a Jordache commercial: tall, blonde, and green-eyed. She was definitely "Beverly Hills 90210" material. In short, she was . . .

"Wow!"

Nobody heard him say it, but Nick couldn't help letting that little exclamation slip from his lips.

Rex and his Barbie clones strode past Jordan and Renee as if they were hallway mannequins. But they did manage to stop in front of Nick.

"Dude," Rex said as he nodded toward the new girl. "This is Jessica. She's gonna hang with us at the Battle."

"Cool," Nick managed to croak through a mouth that had suddenly turned as dry as the Sahara. He caught Renee shooting him a pained look, so he shifted his face from her view.

"What're we doing slumming around here?" Rex said as he glanced over to Jordan and Renee. He flashed them his best put-down look, a Rex speciality. "Let's go over to my place and chill," he said.

"Fer sure," Babs and Jessica recited in perfect, mindless unison. Renee thought they sounded like electronic dolls. Given the chance, she was sure she could short-circuit their little wires in two seconds flat—maybe less.

"That sounds cool!" Nick answered. Again he almost caught Renee's eye, and again he quickly shifted his line of vision. When you're playing Benedict Arnold, one thing you don't want is to check in with Betsy Ross.

Rex put his arm around Nick and pulled him along the hallway. "A little advice, Nickster . . ." He made sure he spoke loud enough so Renee and Jordan could hear. "When you're cool, everyone else is a wanna-be . . . very uncool to hang out with wanna-bes."

Renee stared after them in disbelief. "'Wanna-bes'?"

"Wanna-be what?" Jordan asked, once again missing the point by a mile.

Renee, on the other hand, got the point. And it landed right in her gut. OK, so maybe she wasn't going to win Miss Popularity, or maybe she needed a few more curves in a few more places, but at least she had more than golden curls and hot air beneath a designer hat. So how could her good buddy, Nicholas Martin, suddenly treat her so badly?

Renee wasn't the only one puzzled by Nick's little performance.

Derrick Cryder leaned against the wall, gnawing on a toothpick. He had just seen the second act of this little show, and he didn't like it any better than the first.

Obviously, something had to be done. . . .

FIVE
So Long, McGee

My spaceship touched down on the planet Gobbley-
Goop with a low whine and a loud KER-SPLAT!!
The whine came from my turbo thrusters, but the
KER-SPLAT had me completely baffled . . . until I
hopped out of the capsule and sank up to my
aroma-free armpits in banana cream filling.

Immediately I did what any peace ambassador and
part-time junk food junkie would do: I ate like a pig!

True, I was sent by the Federation of Planets to
establish peace on this war-torn world—but we are
talking about banana cream pies here . . . with gold-
en graham cracker crusts!

Still, my feeding frenzy was short-lived.

"Look out, Mr. Ambassador!"

I spun around just in time to see half a dozen
lemon meringue pies flying at me. I had two choices:

A. Duck.
B. Leap up and chow down as many of those pal-
atable projectiles as possible.

Being the health-conscious hero that I am, I chose to duck instead of leap (mostly 'cause my leaper was a bit overloaded from all those banana creams I'd been putting down). "What's going on?" I screamed as the delectable delicacies sailed over my head.

"It's the Pie-droids!" a young man to my left screamed. "They're attacking us with everything they've got!" From the mashed potatoes and carrots smeared across his face, I immediately knew he was a member of that much-loved and well-respected race, the Vegetable-flingers. Much loved by everyone but the Pie-droids, that is.

For centuries the Pie-droids and Vegetable-flingers had been at war; for generations their children had wakened to the vicious sound of flying vegetables and plummeting pies. And now here I was, McGee the Marvelous, Ambassador of Goodwill, Perpetrator of Peace (and a dropout of Weight Watchers), trying to restore order.

That was the good news. The bad news was I was standing directly between the two warring armies.

"Incoming!" a Pie-droid to my right yelled. Suddenly ten tablespoons of corn and four heads of overcooked broccoli exploded at my feet.

As the vegetables cascaded around me I jumped to my left foot, then my right, then my left again . . . I looked like some crazy tap dancer. So I grabbed the cane and top hat I keep in my briefcase just for such occasions and began an impressive song-and-dance routine of "Old Folks at Home." Stephen C. Foster couldn't have done it better himself.

"Way down upon de Swanee Ribber,
Far, far away . . ."

"Stop it!" the Pie-droids screamed.

"Dere's wha my heart is turning ebber,
Dere's wha de old folks stay . . ."

"Make him quit!" the Vegetable-flingers cried. But nothing would stop these talented tootsies or silence my sensational singing:

"All up and down de whole creation
Sadly I roam,
Still longing for de old plantation,
And for de old folks at home!"

The vegetables came harder and faster.
So did the pies.
It was like a giant dessert and salad bar . . . all you can eat, all at once, all raining down on top of me. But I wasn't worried. How could I be? I'm the hero of this story. Besides, it was all part of my plan. It was why I was chosen in the first place. I'll explain more as soon as I'm done with the chorus. All together now:

"All de world am sad and dreary,
Da-da-da-da-deee . . ."

"Daaa-da-dee's" are always good when you forget the words. And, thanks to all the banging my beanie was getting from the zinging zucchini and

pelting pies, my memory—along with the rest of my brain—was going fast. Still, being the fearless hero I am, I pressed on.

"Please!" they cried, holding their ears in agony. "Please stop."

But I just kept singing and dancing. "Second chorus!" I shouted. "Everybody join in if you know the words."

"All right! All right!" they cried, dropping to their knees, tears streaming down their cheeks. "We'll do anything you say!"

"Anything?" I beamed, still tapping the paint off my cartoon tootsies.

"Anything," they shouted back.

"You'll stop this senseless war?"

They hesitated.

I sang louder.

"All right, all right!" they screamed. "We'll stop fighting. Just—just quit that awful noise!"

I came to a stop. Both sides broke into applause— then a standing ovation. (I knew I was good, but not that good.)

Over the next few days, we began the delicate phase of disarmament. But we didn't destroy the weapons. No sir. Not the way worldwide hunger is spreading. Instead the Veggie-flingers donated their wholesome goodies to hundreds of Junk Food Rehab Centers. They figured junk food addicts from around the country would come in and trade their chips and candies for broccoli and cauliflower. (Yeah, right. Like these people are in touch with reality. . . .)

"But what about the pies?" the Veggie-flingers

asked suspiciously. "If we give up our vegetables, what are the Pie-droids willing to do with their pies?"

I flashed them my famous Ambassador smile. "Trust me."

The following day my spacecraft was ready to leave for home. It was a little tricky getting off the ground with all the deep-dish apples, lemon meringues, and coconut creams stored on board, but I was willing to take the risk if it meant bringing permanent peace to this troubled world.

With a mighty K-WOOOOSH! I took off. Now it was just me and the thousands of tons of sugar-saturated, fabulously fruity, candy-coated calories. But that's OK, somebody had to make the sacrifice. It's a tough job (burp) but somebody's gotta (belch) do it. (Ahhh . . .)

Now I could settle back and enjoy the fact that, once again, a mightily magnificent job was masterminded by the marvelous—

Whoa!!

Suddenly my spaceship dissolved, the pies vanished, and I was back on the sketch pad where I had just enjoyed this little fantasy. As I wiped the make-believe crumbs from my mouth, my beautiful baby blues caught a glimpse of Nick outside the window. Good timing! By the looks of things I could use some touch-up paint on my tap dancing tootsies—not to mention a little tummy tuck around the ol' pie disposal unit. (Good thing he'd sketched me in erasable pencil.)

The best I figured—and believe me, nothing's

*finer than my fancy figuring (unless, of course,
you're talking dill pickles smothered in chocolate
sauce, one of my all-time favorite munchies)—ol'
Nick had been hanging out with Rex the Wreck
again. Personally, I'd like to lock old Rexy boy in a
room and throw away the room! Right now, though,
it looked like I had a more important mission than
ridding the world of Rex the Mess. From the looks
of my buddy, I knew it was time to launch "Opera-
tion Save Nick from Himself."*

A minute later Nicholas burst into his room like a
kid looking for eggs on Easter. He'd just gotten a
little chocolate stain on his white T-shirt, but the
way he was panicking you'd think they'd just out-
lawed Nintendo.

"Mo-o-o-o-om!" he screamed as he rushed to the
mirror and anxiously rubbed at the tiny stain with
his washrag.

Mom was right behind him. "You know, Honey,
toothpaste and bleach will take that stain right
out." She reached for his shirt. "Just take this off
and I'll—"

But Nicholas yanked away. "I can take care of it
myself, Mom!" That kind of behavior and lip would
have normally gotten Nick grounded for life, but
his mom was so surprised, she just stared at her
obnoxious offspring. "Well . . . OK." She headed
back to the door, then her face lit up like a Christmas tree. "Oh, Nick," she said, spinning back to
him. "Guess what?"

Nick sighed. Somehow he figured he'd know
"what" whether he guessed it or not. He was right.

"Your dad doesn't know it yet, but I'm getting out his old saxophone. They're going to ask him to do a little jam session at the Battle of the Bands. Won't that be . . . cool?" Her voice trailed off as she looked for a reaction, maybe even a grin.

Nick gave her nothing, except for a roll of the eyes and a little groan. "Oh, yeah, cool—like being hit in the head with a glacier."

Once again Mom wasn't exactly sure what to think about this new Nick, so she just gave him a weak smile and headed out the door.

Nick turned his attention back to the stain. "Good job," he sighed as he kept rubbing at it. "I might as well have just drooled on myself!"

Well, it was time to set the kid straight. Time to share my intelligently insightful intellect. I hopped off the sketch pad and onto the drawing table.

"Come on, Nick," I said. "That's only a plain white T-shirt, more commonly known as under-wear!"

"McGeeeee," Nick returned impatiently, "it's the only cool shirt I have!"

"Hey! What about that other one—the one that says 'Cartoons are our friends'?"

"Get real, McGee. It might as well say, 'I'm a geek and proud of it.'"

I couldn't believe my ears. "You used to love that shirt!" I cried.

"That was before," Nick said as he whirled away from the mirror.

"Before what?" I demanded.

He just shrugged.

48

"You mean, before you got . . . cool?" I was really beginning to hate that word.

"Well . . . yeah," Nick answered. Before I knew it he had stalked into the closet and started rummaging through his clothes. "There's nothing here!" he whined. "Nothing at all!"

I began pacing back and forth on the art table. "Kid, you're out of control!" I called. "That 'hair-for-brains' Rexster has made you somebody else! You're bagging on your family and your friends and—"

"Hang it up, McGee!" Nick's voice echoed from inside the closet. Finally he appeared in the doorway, his finger pointing accusingly at me. "Who gave you the right to tell me what to do?"

"Nobody's telling you—"

"I'm the one who created you!"

"Well, yeah, but—"

"Out of nothing!"

"Sure, but—"

"Remember??"

I was lucky to get a word in edgewise . . . or sideways . . . or on its head. "But I'm your best friend," I fired back. "I have privileges!"

Nick fidgeted uncomfortably. I waited.

He leaned against the door and shoved his hands into his pockets. "I'm not so sure of that anymore . . . ," he said, not looking at me.

"WHAT??" I couldn't believe my ears. I stuck my finger into them and gave a good shake. Nothing came out but your usual killer moths, vampire bats, and flying UFOs. (I tell you, I've got to stop watching those late-night TV movies.)

"Draw me some Q-Tips," I continued. "I thought I heard you say . . . we're not friends anymore."

"That's right," Nick fired back. "Drawing cartoons is uncool for a guy my age! Cartoons are for kids!"

It was like he'd punched me in the gut. I couldn't catch my breath. If Nicky quit drawing me—if we quit being friends—it would be curtains, it would mean "Bye-bye McGee." And we ain't talkin' vacation to Disneyland. We're talking your basic "So long," "I'm history," "No more clever comebacks and irresistible insights." In short, I'd become nothing but another drawing on another piece of paper.

"Say it ain't so, kid!" I cried. "Say it ain't so!"

I waited for him to break into his world-famous grin and tell me it was all just a bad joke. Instead, Nick slowly turned his back on me.

And then he said it.

"Just go away. Leave me alone, McGee."

My colors started to fade.

"Nicholas . . ." I tried not to let the hurt come out in my voice. But my incredible wit began to grow witless, my keen intellect began to grow dim, and I started to panic.

"Nicholas . . . ?"

But my little buddy wouldn't turn to help. Any minute the worst of all worsts would happen. I, the magnificently marvelous McGee would become . . . gulp! . . . boring. After that . . . well, after that there was nothing left but cartoon oblivion.

"Nicholas!"

Suddenly my feet started moving. Before I knew it I was heading for the drawing pad. I couldn't help myself. Something was pulling me toward it.

As I stepped onto the paper I glanced at my hands. They were barely visible. Everything about me was fading.

I tried to think of something clever to say, but the cleverness was gone. My brain was going to sleep. I could no longer think.

I was lying down on the pad now. I tried to sit up, but I no longer had the energy to move. I was stuck to the paper for good. With my last ounce of energy I turned my head toward the boy standing across the room. I thought I knew him but I wasn't sure. I wanted to call out his name, but I could no longer remember it.

And then . . .

There was nothing.

SIX
Too Cool to Be Real

"C'mon, Jamie, move it!" Sarah yelled up the stairs. "You're gonna make us late!"

"All right, all right," Jamie's voice echoed from above.

"I'm supposed to meet Tina and a couple of the girls from the team at 4:00," Sarah complained. "If you want to tag along that's OK, but not if you're going to make me late."

"All right, all right," Jamie repeated as she scrambled down the steps. On her head was a bright, neon pink bicycle helmet.

"What are you doing with that?" Sarah demanded.

"It's what I wear when you drive."

"Cute," Sarah said scornfully. "Now let's get going. You know how hard it is to find parking at the mall this time of day."

Half an hour later, Sarah and Jamie rushed through the mall toward Yogurt Yums, the Saturday afternoon gathering place for the Eastfield high-school crowd. Sarah spotted Tina and a couple of other girls from the tennis team sitting at one of the tables, waiting for her. They were putting down a couple of scoops of the no-fat, no-cholesterol, no-taste treat. Sarah raised her hand and started to call to them when suddenly . . .

She heard a giggle. Out of the corner of her eye she caught a couple of cheerleaders laughing with some football jocks. No biggie. A typical, everyday sight: airheads with bicep-brains. Except for one small difference.

One of the jocks was Morgan Jefferson!

"Ohhh, not now!" Sarah groaned as she reached out to grab Jamie.

"Ow!" Jamie cried as she was yanked to an abrupt stop. "What are you trying to do, give me whiplash?"

Sarah didn't have time to explain. In spite of the school paper's photo, she had managed to keep her identity as a tennis player a secret from Morgan. In fact, things were going really well between the two of them . . . but it could all end, right this moment, if he discovered she was a part of the loser crowd. She didn't have time to explain any of that; she just had time to do something drastic—like get out of there, fast!

She spun Jamie around and started toward the nearest exit, then she heard:

"Hey, Sarah!" It was Morgan. He'd spotted her and now, all smiles and waves, he started toward her. Sarah gave him a nervous smile and a half-hearted wave. She glanced quickly toward Tina. It was just as she feared. Tina had heard Sarah's name and was looking around. Bingo! Their eyes connected. Sarah looked away as if she hadn't seen her. But it was too late, and they both knew it.

She looked back to Morgan. He was nearly there.

"Hi!" He grinned. "Blown up any more schools lately?"

Sarah laughed uncomfortably as she threw another look to Tina. Great, just great. Tina and her tennis friends were rising to their feet. Sarah knew what was coming next.

"You going to the game Friday night?" Morgan asked.

But Sarah didn't hear. She was too busy praying that the ground would open up and swallow her whole.

"Sarah?" he repeated.

"Huh?"

"Can you make it to our game Friday?"

"Well, uh, I . . ." She thought she sounded like a babbling fool. She was right. As Tina and the team started toward her she wondered if this was what the captain of the *Titanic* felt when he saw the iceberg coming.

"I was wondering," Morgan continued, "if you'd—"

"Uh . . . I have to go now," Sarah interrupted. "Come on Jamie." She gave Jamie another yank and started toward the exit. Any exit.

"Ow!" Jamie cried, yanking her hand out of Sarah's grip and planting her feet like a stubborn mule.

Morgan tried again. "I . . . was just wondering if

you'd like to go out for a Coke or something after the game?"

"Uh . . ."

"Sarah?" Tina called out, a little puzzled, as she and the team approached.

"Uh . . ."

"Sarah??" They were practically there!

And then, just to make things worse, one of the cheerleaders, Mary Lynn, the class barracuda, suddenly appeared next to Morgan. She put her hand on his shoulder and flashed Sarah a smile so sugarcoated it would make your teeth rot. "Hey, Morgan," she giggled. "I didn't know you knew our little tennis-team captain."

Sarah gulped. She wasn't sure where to look. To Morgan? Or her friends? But Mary Lynn wasn't finished yet. She leaned a fist on her cocked hip. "So tell me, Sarah, you girls planning on winning any matches this year?"

"Hey, Sarah." Tina gave her a put-out look as she arrived. She could tell Sarah was embarrassed, and she had a sneaky feeling she knew the reason.

"Well, speak of the devil," Mary Lynn gloated. "If it isn't the rest of the losers."

Sarah tried to speak but nothing came out. She wanted to say it was all a terrible mistake, that there was a girl who looked just like her on the tennis team. She wanted to deny that she ever knew Tina. She wanted to race right out and buy Mary Lynn a ticking time bomb for Christmas. But nothing happened. She just stood there, her face on fire.

"I . . ." She turned to Morgan. "I'll see you in chemistry."

With that she turned and left, dragging the protesting Jamie all the way.

Mary Lynn looked on in satisfaction.

Morgan watched in confusion.

And Tina? She stood there, hurt in her eyes, feeling the pain that only comes when your best friend stabs you in the back.

By the night of "The Battle of the Bands," Nicholas had changed everything: his clothes, his friends, his room. Gone were all his neat inventions. Gone were all his McGee drawings. In fact, you had to look hard just to find his drawing table. Now it was hidden under a stack of heavy metal CDs, which, of course, were Rex's. Nick's allowance (not to mention his mom and dad) would never let him start a collection of "that kind of music."

Nick was at his favorite spot, in front of the mirror, when there was a knock on the door.

"Come in," he called as he splashed on some cologne.

Mom and Dad entered. Nick nearly dropped the cologne bottle when he saw them. They were decked out, from head to toe, in sixties getups. Dad wore bell-bottom jeans, a checkered shirt, and a flowered vest. Then, of course, there was the hair combed straight down over the forehead. And what "Beatles look" would be complete without John Lennon glasses?

But as bad as Dad looked, Mom looked worse. First there was the neon green miniskirt, then the love beads—and let's not forget those ever-white and ever-popular go-go boots!

"How do we look?" Mom asked with a broad grin.

Nick suppressed a gag. "This is a joke, right? Nobody's wearing costumes. You're not really gonna go like that, are you?" (Maybe Rex was right—maybe his parents really *were* from another universe.)

"Of course we are," Mom said. "Your principal thought it would be fun if we dressed up in a sixties look."

"Yeah." Nick fumbled for the words. "But couldn't you just wear a . . . a peace sign or something?"

Dad put his arm around Nicholas's shoulder. "What's the matter, Son?" he chuckled. "Don't wanna be seen with half the members of the 'Mamas and Papas'?"

The situation called for drastic action. Unfortunately Nick didn't have a clue what that would be. Changing his name and plastic surgery came to mind, but none of those could be done in the next hour or so. Well, at least there was one way out.

"Now that you mention it, Dad, I'm gonna walk over there with my friends."

"Oh, Nick," Mom said, a little disappointed, "I thought we'd be going as a family."

Nicholas plopped down on his bed, avoiding their eyes. "I see you guys all the time," he whined. "I'd rather go with my friends."

"We understand that," Dad said as he sat next to him. "We just assumed that tonight, since your mom and I have been asked to be hosts—"

Nick's patience broke. "That's another thing!" he blurted out as he jumped up from the bed. "Why do they have to make such a big deal of this twenty-five-year thing anyway?" He paced to the other side of the room. "Come Monday, every kid in school is gonna be laughing at me and saying, 'There goes Nick, son of the world's oldest living teenyboppers.'"

Silence fell over the room. Mom and Dad exchanged worried glances. Worried and hurt. Finally Dad spoke up. "Are you . . . embarrassed by us, Son?"

Nick paced faster. "It . . . it's just not cool to have your parents show up at the biggest event of the year! And to show up like—like this . . . It's, like, the ultimate embarrassment!"

Again Mom and Dad traded looks. Nick had never said he was embarrassed by them before. This was supposed to be fun—a joke. Everybody was supposed to laugh. But right now, laughing was the last thing any of them had on their minds.

At last Dad gave a deep sigh and walked over to Nick. "We've always said there are some decisions we're gonna have to let you make on your own." He placed a hand gently on his son's shoulder. "If you don't want to go with us, I guess it's your choice."

Mom and Dad turned and walked toward the door. They looked back one last time. Dad tried to smile as he said, "We'll do our best to stay out of your way tonight, Son."

There was a knot in Nick's chest the size of a tennis ball. A part of him wanted to say something—to tell them it was OK, and he would be proud of whatever they did. But that part had gotten awfully small—and it was growing smaller by the minute.

Instead, he swallowed hard and said nothing.

SEVEN
Getting Real

Cars surged through the parking lot like ants with headlights. Squadrons of junior highers piled out of the doors and swarmed up the steps, passing beneath a banner that read "25th Annual Battle of the Bands."

Tonight was the night. The "battle" was on, and Eastfield Junior High gymnasium was the war zone. Inside, the hallway was swarming with teens and teachers. Everyone milled about or lined up at the tables to buy tickets.

Besides the millers and the liners, there were the leaners. Among them, Rex and Nick. They had the best leaning spot in the hall. Anybody coming through the doors had to see them: shades down, decked out in the coolest duds, the hottest chicks dangling from their arms—they couldn't be missed. Any second they expected the Webster folks to show up, take their picture, and put it in the dictionary under the new and improved definition of "cool."

Usually people who came through the doors wouldn't even rate a nod from this hip foursome. But Rex was feeling particularly generous this evening. Occasionally he would actually tip his shades when a fellow brother of coolness passed.

"Rex," the beautiful Babs squealed, "you are, like, so *très* cool!"

Though he had no idea what she meant, Rex grunted in agreement. After all she'd used the word "cool," so it must be good.

"So, dude," Nick asked as he gave an awkward thumbs-up to another cool passerby. "When are we, like, going in?"

"Chill, dude," Rex answered with a shrug. "We'll get around to it. Meantime, there's only one thing I wanna do . . ."

"What's that?"

"Be seen, bud. Be seen. It's what makes life cool."

Babs and Jessica giggled with delight at Rex's deep insight. Just then a particular group of uncool teens walked by. Among them were Renee and Jordan. Nick's eyes followed Renee. She looked kind of nice . . . sweet . . . even pretty. Unfortunately nice, sweet, and pretty don't qualify as "cool."

"Hi, Nick," she said with a sad smile as she passed. Nick managed a little nod.

"Like . . . who was that?" Babs asked with a sarcastic laugh. "Little Miss Muffet?" Rex and Jessica snickered with her as they glanced at Nick.

Nicholas swallowed hard. "A friend," he said, forcing his own kind of half laugh.

"You mean, *former* friend," Rex corrected.

Nick hesitated, then nodded. He wasn't sure why, but he was beginning to get a headache. Maybe it was the shades. Maybe it was all this work of being cool. Or maybe it was something else . . .

Before Nick had time to give it any more thought, Rex spotted somebody down at the far end of the hall. "Watch this," he said with an evil grin. He pulled out a marker from his coat and crossed over to the row of lockers.

Nicholas looked down the hallway to see who Rex had spotted. It was Philip. When Nick looked back, Rex had just finished writing the word *Geek* across Philip's locker. He stuffed the pen back into his pocket and quickly returned to his leaning position against the wall.

All eyes watched as Philip approached. Babs and Jessica started snickering. Then Philip spotted his locker.

The snickers grew louder.

Philip looked up. There was no missing the hurt in his eyes as he looked to Rex, then Babs, then Jessica, and finally . . . to Nicholas.

Nick looked down. He felt his jaw tighten. That tennis ball knot returned to his chest—only now it felt as big as a basketball.

Philip started to speak—he wanted to say something to his old buddy, but nothing came. Instead, he just blinked back the moisture filling his eyes, lowered his own head, and walked past without a word.

The basketball had risen to Nick's throat. He tried to swallow it back, but with little success.

62

"Come on, let's go in," Babs pleaded as she tugged at Rex's arm. "I spent, like, a whole month's allowance on this outfit. I wanna show it off!"

"Yeah, sure, it's cool," Rex agreed, giving her a quick squeeze. "Come on." He signaled for Nick and Jessica to follow.

Nicholas turned toward the ticket table, but Rex immediately grabbed him by the collar. "Not that way, dude," he scorned. "That's the entrance for people who have to buy tickets."

"But . . ." Nick looked confused. "Don't we have to buy tickets?"

"No way, bro!" Rex chuckled as he glanced around for onlookers. Then, quickly, he herded Nick and the girls down a side hallway. "You're with me, remember?"

"Oh, yeah," Nick muttered with a worried half smile. "Cool . . ." Nicholas's headache was getting worse. So was that basketball in his stomach or in his throat or wherever it was. Since when was ripping off the school and not paying your way "cool"?

As they ambled down the hallway, Nick kept glancing over his shoulder until Rex grabbed him and dragged him down a flight of stairs. As they descended the steps Nicholas had the distinct feeling he was sinking lower and lower—in more ways than one.

Moments later the four party-crashers appeared in the gym behind the bleachers. Rex strutted into the open like he had just outfoxed the CIA, FBI, and Agatha Christie all at the same time. Nick, on the other hand, sort of backed in with his head down. It had been a long time since he'd felt so rotten. He glanced around, and his eyes widened.

Either the gymnasium was really decorated or they were caught in some "Star Trek" time warp. The whole gym looked like a hangout from the late sixties, complete with surfboards, cutout palm trees, and a cardboard '68 Corvette convertible.

"Prehistoric, dude," Rex whispered.

Much to Nick's relief, nobody seemed to notice their back alley entrance. Nobody, that is, except Derrick. He was leaning against a wall doing his usual toothpick-chewing routine when he saw them come in. He knew Rex, so he wasn't surprised to see him make a thief's entrance. But when he saw Nick following, Derrick threw down his toothpick in disgust.

As the Cool-R-Us troop climbed up on the bleachers to sit, Mrs. Pryce stepped to the microphone. A ripple of chuckles wafted through the crowd when they saw her outfit. It probably had something to do with the yellow glow-in-the-dark miniskirt she wore.

"Testing . . . ah, hum . . . testing . . ."

WAAAAIIIIINGGGGGGGGGG!

That, of course, was feedback. After several seconds and lots of knob turning, the earsplitting sound finally faded.

Mrs. Pryce stepped back up to the microphone. "In a few minutes," she said, "we'll be ready to start our Endless Summer Battle of the Bands. I guarantee you, it will be very . . . groovy." She chuckled at her humor. Everyone else groaned. Everyone, that is, except Babs and Jessica. They

64

were too busy critiquing the fashion scene to pay attention.

"Did you see what Sherry Nunnally is wearing?" Babs asked. "Don't you just want to gag?"

Jessica, whose vocabulary was usually limited to "oh my gosh" and "cool," managed to squeeze out a few giggles in agreement.

"Ouuu," Babs said, pointing across the room, "check out the Neanderthals!"

Nicholas's eyes followed her finger. He wished they hadn't. One of her ultramanicured, super-long, hot-red-polish-with-a-white-swirl-in-the-middle-of-the-nail fingers was jabbing right at his mom and dad. They were crossing toward Mrs. Pryce and yucking it up with some of the kids.

Before Nick could answer, Babs changed the subject again. "Nobody's seeing my outfit up here," she complained. "Can't we go mingle now?"

"Not if you wanna be cool," Rex answered. "When you're cool, you find some out-of-the-way place like this and let the minglers come to you."

Suddenly a firm hand gripped Nick's shoulder. He whipped around to see Derrick Cryder standing directly over him. Rex saw him, too. Immediately he ceased being the King of Cool. "Uh . . . h-hi, Derrick!" he stuttered.

Derrick grunted a nod. Then motioned to Nick. "The squid here and I need a little talk."

"Sure, Derrick," Rex said with an eager nod. "Whatever you say." He started to rise until Derrick flashed him a frown.

"Just the Nick . . . in private."

65

"Oh . . . yeah . . . sure . . ." Rex sat back down, looking a little deflated.

Nicholas glanced about as he rose and silently followed Derrick down the bleachers and into a deserted locker room. All sorts of messy thoughts went through his head, but they all narrowed down to one: *What am I doing alone with Derrick Cryder?!!*

A year ago he would have known it meant instant pain, maybe even death. But ever since their little Christmas encounter Derrick had given up the bully business. Of course, he could be trying to make a comeback . . . and Nick could always be the first victim in his return engagement.

As they entered the room and the door swung shut, Derrick pointed forcefully to the nearest bench. Nick obeyed without speaking, without even thinking—well, except for wondering if his parents' health insurance would cover him for whatever was coming.

Derrick stepped toward him and growled, "What're you doin' hanging out with that loser?" He jabbed his finger back toward the door.

"Loser?" Nick croaked. "He . . . he's the most popular kid in school, Derrick!"

Derrick scowled harder.

Nick gave a swallow and continued. "And when I hang with him, I'm popular, too."

"Popular?!" Derrick shouted as he slammed his hand against a nearby locker. "I thought you knew what was important!"

"I do," Nick said, even more nervous over Derrick's outburst.

"You *did*," Derrick hissed. He shoved his face into Nick's. "When you stood up to me last Christmas—when you told me about God—then you knew something. But now . . . now I'm not sure you know anything, Martin."

He stepped back and looked down at Nicholas, who swallowed again . . . or at least tried. When you're going to die, sometimes it's hard to find anything to swallow. But it wasn't Derrick's style to play destruction derby with people's faces anymore. Instead, he reached out and removed Nick's shades. "Be who you are, man," he said softly.

Nick looked up and blinked.

"These things don't fit you," Derrick said as he calmly folded up the glasses and stuck them into Nick's shirt pocket. Then, without a word, he turned and walked out the door.

Suddenly Nick was alone. All alone. He sat for a long moment trying to figure out what had just happened. Finally he stood up and started to adjust his hair. Then he saw it. His reflection in the mirror. And a sudden shock went through him. That wasn't him. It couldn't be. The black vest, black shirt, black pants . . . no way.

What *was* he doing? Who was he trying to be?

Derrick's voice rang loudly in his ears: "Be who you are, man." Nick slowly sank onto the bench.

EIGHT
Clear Vision

About the same time Nick and Rex were sneaking into the "Battle," the high schoolers across town were having a battle of their own—on the gridiron. Well, maybe "battle" isn't the right word; "massacre" is more like it. By halftime the visiting team had more points on their side of the scoreboard than most teams score in an entire season, while the hometown boys just couldn't seem to get rid of that big fat "0" on their side.

As the marching band stumbled out onto the field for halftime entertainment, Sarah and Jamie stood in the long line at the concession stand. It hadn't been Sarah's best week. She'd completely avoided Morgan; Tina had completely avoided her; and now she had to baby-sit her tagalong sister for the evening. Yes sir, on the scale of one to ten, this week was definitely somewhere in the minus column.

"Sarah." Jamie tugged at her shirt.

"Stop it," Sarah whispered out of the corner of

her mouth. She smiled at a couple of passing kids, doing her best to pretend Jamie didn't exist. But if there's one thing Jamie's good at, it's making sure she isn't ignored.

"Sarah—"

"You were supposed to keep three steps behind me!" Sarah scowled harshly. "What if somebody sees you're with me?"

"Let's just get the food," Jamie stated.

"You have any suggestions?" Sarah shot back. "I'm not Moses, and this crowd's not gonna part for us, no matter how much you whine."

"I wish we'd stayed at home. We're missing the 'My Little Pony Meets Batman' special," she sulked. "Just 'cause you want to see Mr. Hunk in action."

"Morgan has nothing to do with me being here." The line moved up a person. "I told you," Sarah continued, "it's all over between us."

"Good thing," Jamie agreed. "I've never seen a team throw so many interruptions in my life."

"That's 'interceptions,'" Sarah corrected. "And since when do you know a football game from hop-scotch?"

"I know a failed thirty-three green, right-split reverse when I see one."

Sarah stopped and gaped at her sister. She wasn't sure if Jamie knew what she was talking about or if she was just bluffing—it was hard to tell with Jamie. But Sarah did know one thing: the team had played an entire half, and Morgan hadn't gone in once.

Sarah and Jamie arrived at the counter and

made their purchases as, out on the field, the marching band finished their halftime show. Everyone seemed grateful that the noise was over. There was something about all that drum pounding and out-of-tune playing that made people appreciate silence.

"So, where's your Morgan, anyway?" Jamie asked.

"I don't know." Sarah shrugged sadly. "It doesn't matter . . . not anymore."

A loud cheer erupted from the stands. Cheerleaders shouted, fans clapped, and, unfortunately, the band started to play as the teams raced back onto the field.

Armed with a corn dog and a couple of slices of rubbery pizza, Sarah and Jamie made their way back toward their seats. To one side was the grandstand, which was full of noisy and excited people. To the other side were the players on the sideline, yelling and pumping each other up for the second-half kickoff.

Sarah nibbled on her corn dog. Jamie ate her pizza, shoving it into her mouth like it was on a conveyor belt.

"Jamie!" Sarah scolded. "You're not supposed to eat pizza like a paper shredder! At least breathe once in a while!"

Jamie stopped long enough to catch her breath, then started in again. "Mit's meefa omma memamama mif mwam mwa." (Translation: "It's my pizza, and I can eat it any way I want.")

Suddenly there was a voice from the sideline. "Hey! Sarah!"

Sarah turned. "Morgan!" she gasped.

Yep, there he was—her ex-heartthrob . . . on crutches. "What happened?" she exclaimed.

"It looks worse than it is—just a twisted ankle. But it was enough to keep me outta the game." Then, spotting Jamie, he gave her a quick chuck under the chin. "Hey, how ya doin', short stuff?"

"Miff mumms mraumms," Jamie mumbled between bites.

The crowd started to roar—a sure sign that the kickoff was about to take place. Sarah and Morgan turned toward the field. Horns blared, cymbals crashed, and cheerleaders cartwheeled as the ball went sailing through the air and the Eastfield receiver moved under to catch it.

Cheers exploded as he caught the ball. Groans followed as he slipped and fell.

"Not going too well, is it?" Sarah asked meekly.

"Oh, there's still time." Morgan shrugged. "Swivel Hips Rick just has to settle down some. He'll do it. You'll see."

There was a moment of silence as Sarah and Morgan tried to figure out what to say next. Finally they both started, at the same time:

"Listen, I want to—"

"Morgan, I'm really—"

They both gave nervous laughs.

"Go ahead," Morgan offered.

"No, you," Sarah insisted, grateful that she wouldn't have to go first.

"Well . . ." Morgan took a deep breath. "I just want to say I know why you're avoiding me, and you're absolutely right!"

"I am?" Sarah asked, a little confused.

"Absolutely," he said with a nod. "I was a total jerk, making fun of the tennis team like that."

"But—"

Morgan held out his hand and continued. "I know you guys are really trying. Besides, what kind of idiot would make fun of people who are giving it their best shot?"

Sarah was caught off balance. Before she had a chance to answer, the bleachers suddenly erupted into cheers. Fans leaped from their seats. Sarah and Morgan spun around to see what had happened.

"All right!" Morgan shouted, "First down! Way to go, Rick!" Then he turned back to Sarah. "Anyway, I just wanted to say I was sorry and I can understand why you don't want to be around me."

Sarah just stared, mouth agape. She wanted to say something, but at the moment nothing came to mind. Nothing at all.

Fortunately, Jamie always has something to say. "Close your mouth, Sarah, or you'll catch flies." (Good ol' Jamie.)

The barb brought Sarah back to reality. "I . . . uh . . ." She shook her head. "That's OK, Morgan. I'm the one who owes you an apology."

"Me?" Morgan asked.

"I had no business deceiving you—pretending to be something I'm not."

"You never deceiv—"

"Sure I did." Sarah took a gulp of air. It was true confessions time—something she'd been thinking about the whole week and something she finally had to get off her chest. "I should have told you right off the bat I was on the team, but I was too embarrassed. And because of that I not only lost you, I lost my best friend . . ." She forced out a little laugh. "Guess that makes me a loser all the way around."

"No," Morgan interrupted. "You're not a loser. Not to me."

Sarah looked up. There was no mistaking the sincerity in his eyes. Once again they were interrupted by the roar of the crowd. They looked out to the field just in time to see Swivel Hips Rick fire off a long, beautiful pass.

"All right!" Morgan cheered. "Way to go, Ricky!"

They continued to watch as the ball sailed long and high . . . right into the other team's arms for another perfect interception. The crowd groaned.

Morgan could only shake his head. "They're stomping us. I can't look—it's too embarrassing."

"I know the feeling," Sarah teased. "But don't worry, you'll get used to it."

Morgan looked up. For a moment she thought she'd gone too far. She wasn't sure if he was going to yell or laugh. Then she saw it: a grin forming on his lips. She broke into a broader smile.

Finally he spoke. "So when's your next match, Martin?"

"Why?"

"So I can be there and get more pointers on how to lose," he teased.

"You!" she said, giving him a poke in the ribs, and then another.

"Whoa!" he cried, almost losing his balance. She

had to reach out and catch him or he and his crutches would have gone down for sure. And then somehow, some way, he had taken her hand . . . and he didn't let go.

Sarah beamed.

Jamie watched the whole thing. For once in her life she said nothing. She simply shook her head in disgust, wondering if there was any way to skip being a teenager.

Nick was suffering big-time teen pangs himself. He was leaning against the gym wall, watching everyone having fun. For some reason he felt like he was barely there. He felt like some sort of space alien watching while everyone else laughed and had a great time.

Mrs. Pryce was back at the microphone. "All right . . . are you groovy guys and gals hip to start the Big Battle?"

Hoots and cheers answered her question.

"OK, then, it's my pleasure to introduce two former Eastfield students who, twenty-five years ago tonight, started our very first Battle of the Bands."

Nick wiped the sweat from his forehead. Here it came. He had no doubt that it would be the most embarrassing moment of his life. His only question was, would the humiliation come quickly and mercifully, or would it be dragged out through the entire dance?

Mrs. Pryce continued, "Those two very special people went on to become husband and wife, and they're back with us to host tonight's battle.

Please put your hands together for David and Elizabeth Martin."

Applause filled the gym as Mom and Dad stepped up to the microphone. Nick looked surprised. He thought the kids would fall down laughing—not applaud. He looked around, confused. It—it was almost like they . . . *liked* his dad!

Dad took the microphone as the applause began to fade. "Thank you all very much." He grinned. "You know, Mrs. Pryce, twenty-five years hasn't changed this place much." He gestured toward the wall. "The drinking fountain still doesn't work."

It was a corny joke, but everyone laughed along with it. Everyone but Nick. He still wasn't sure what to do.

Dad continued. "It's a great honor for Elizabeth and me to be here tonight. In a few moments, we're gonna introduce some of the most talented young musicians in all of Eastfield. There will be four bands, each doing a set of fifteen minutes." Applause again filled the room along with some scattered cheers and yells.

"But before we do that . . ." Dad lifted his hand to quiet them. "As one Eastfield Eagle to another, I'd like to offer each of you a special challenge."

The noise died down. Everyone began to listen.

"You know, this is one of the most important times of your life. A lot of what's going to happen to you later on is going to start right here in junior high." He paused a moment to let the point sink in. "So get a good start," he continued. "Believe in yourself, in your family . . . and in friends who really care about you."

The words hit Nick dead center. He knew Dad hadn't planned it that way, but that didn't stop the words from hitting their mark.

"And above all, understand who you are and what you believe in, here," Dad said, touching his heart, "inside. Be yourself. Be the person God made you to be."

Nick felt his face getting a little hot. He looked around again, afraid of what he would see. But his schoolmates were quiet, and all eyes were fixed on Dad. The kids could tell the man meant what he was saying. They knew he believed it and, at least for that moment, they believed it, too.

Come to think of it . . . so did Nick.

"And now," Dad said, suddenly lightening up, "I'll step aside and let the Battle begin!"

The audience cheered. Yelps and catcalls rattled the rafters as Dad made the first introduction: "Starting with the moldy oldie that opened the first battle . . . take it away, The Armadillos!"

But before the audience could break into applause Principal Pryce suddenly reappeared. In her hand was a saxophone.

"Hold on a second, David. You're gonna either love me or hate me for this," she shoved the saxophone into his hands, "but would you do us the honor of blowing a little riff on this first song, just like you did twenty-five years ago?"

Again the audience broke into loud cheers as the curtain opened behind them. There was the band, tuned up and ready to play. For a second Dad protested, but the audience cheered him on until, reluctantly, he clipped the horn to his neck strap and sighed. "Whew . . ." was all he said, but it brought another wave of applause.

He looked back to the band. They were waiting.

Nick quietly bit his lip.

"Well," Dad sighed again, "here goes nothing. You guys ready?"

The players in the band nodded. The drummer clicked off the opening beats with his sticks, and the music began. Dad took a deep breath, put the saxophone to his lips, and started the opening bars. The first few notes were a little weak and self-conscious, but soon Dad was rocking like a pro.

The audience was right with him, cheering and clapping.

Nick couldn't believe his ears—or his heart. He was actually proud of his dad. And the guy wasn't even trying to be anything . . . he was just Dad.

Nicholas glanced over at Mom. She was watching "her man" rip off the tune. She had her hands together like they had frozen in mid-clap, and you could tell from her smile why they were married, why they were such good friends, and why they were such a happy family.

Friends . . . family, Nick thought. *What have I done to them . . . to all of them?*

His eyes moved from Mom to the snack table where Philip, Renee, and Jordan drank punch. They were smiling, laughing, and having a great time. But how could they, the "uncool," be so happy?

What was more, if you could be happy without being cool, what was the point of working so hard to be cool? Come to think of it, how happy had he

been since he moved into the world of "ultracool?"
Oh sure, people had finally begun to notice him.
But was he happy?

Hyperstressed? Maybe.

Guilty? Absolutely.

But happy? No way.

Nick watched Philip. He remembered the eager
look on his face when he'd told Nick about the
computer show. Then there was the memory of
happy-go-lucky Jordan tossing his football into
the air. The guy was always so accepting, always
so happy.

Nicholas glanced over at Rex and his clones.
They looked anything but happy. After all, it was
against the "cool code" to enjoy anything. Feelings
weren't cool, caring wasn't cool, friends weren't
cool, love wasn't cool.

He remembered how nervous he'd been when
Rex was over for dinner and they'd held hands. He
thought about all the love around the table—love
that his family felt toward each other and toward
the Lord. Definitely "uncool," but definitely good.
Very, very good.

He looked back to his dad, still rocking away on
the sax, then to his mom laughing and clapping
. . . and he groaned inwardly. The image of their
expressions when he told them he wasn't going
with them to the Battle of the Bands floated in his
mind. He'd hurt them—a lot.

And finally, there was McGee, his longest and
best friend . . . Nick frowned, a sick feeling in his
gut.

That was it. Nick knew what he had to do. It

wouldn't be easy. And it definitely wouldn't be "cool." But he was going to do it.

Nicholas turned and started toward Rex and the gang.

NINE
Wrapping Up

As Dad's saxophone wailed, Nick's mind raced.

How had he gotten himself into such a mess? More importantly, how was he going to get himself out? However he did it, there was no way he could do it and still look cool. But then, looking cool wasn't such a big deal. Doing the right thing—that was the ticket. And as much as Nick hated to admit it, he knew what that right thing was.

He continued toward Rex, slowly at first. With any luck maybe there'd be a giant earthquake before he arrived. Or a tornado. Shoot, right now he'd settle for a good old-fashioned flash flood. But there was nothing. Just the hooting and hollering of the crowd as Dad continued his sax solo . . . and Nicholas started up the bleachers.

"Hey, dude," Rex shouted as he approached. "Your dad blows a pretty mean 'phone for a fossil." He laughed, giving the cue to Babs and Jessica to follow along. They giggled.

"Yeah," Nick agreed, turning back to look at his dad. "He is pretty good, isn't he?"

Rex continued. "The three of us were thinking about sneaking into the flicks later tonight. What do you say?"

Nicholas turned back to Rex. He had wanted to be like this guy for weeks. He'd wanted people to admire him. He'd wanted girls dangling from his arms. He'd wanted people eating up his every word. But now . . .

Now the price was too high. It wasn't worth forgetting who he was to be someone he wasn't. Well, it was now or never. Nicholas took a deep breath. "Look, Rex, uh . . . thanks for the invite—and for letting me hang out with you—but, uh, I . . . think I've had enough."

There, he'd done it. He'd said no to Rex and yes to who he was. He stood there a second. It was all over, just like that. Finally he started to turn away, but stopped. Something else had to be done. Something to seal the deal, to make sure there was no turning back.

"Oh, and one more thing," Nick said as he turned to Rex. He reached into his pocket and pulled out his sunglasses. "Here. I don't see too well with these on."

He handed them to Rex.

For a moment the guy looked kinda confused. But Nick knew he'd eventually figure it out. So he simply turned and walked back down the bleachers.

Rex watched in astonishment. The look on his face told the whole story. It was clear that nobody had ever turned their back on him—not the great Rexster! Who did this punk think he was, anyway? After all, he'd taken the geek in, shown him the ropes, taught him what it was to be cool . . . given him a chance to be somebody. And now he just walks away?

Rex wanted to say something—he wanted to shout at Nick, tell him what a loser he was, but shouting wasn't cool. Shouting meant you cared. And Rex was too cool to care. Instead, he shut down his emotions and shifted into ultracool. He chuckled to the girls as he shoved the shades into his pocket. "Once a loser, always a loser," he said with a smirk. Babs and Jessica giggled right on cue. Just like always.

Meanwhile, Derrick had seen the whole thing from across the gym. "Way to go, Martin." He smiled to himself. "Way to go."

Nick continued moving through the crowd. It was like he was waking up from a dream. Everything was a blur—the lights, the kids, even the music was a mishmash of sounds. Except for the sax. He stopped beside one of the cardboard decorations on the wall, a Corvette cutout, to watch his dad. Nick grinned. Maybe it wouldn't be so bad to be like him when he grew up. Without, of course, the hair and bell-bottoms.

He turned to look around—and spotted them.

Renee, Philip, and Jordan were clustered together across the room. Nick swallowed hard. They were his friends. At least, they used to be. He'd betrayed them. No question. If they refused to talk to him for the rest of his life, he couldn't blame them.

He turned and started to walk away. He'd already been through one emotional roller coaster. He didn't need another "Maalox moment."

But he'd only taken a few steps before he stopped. With a sigh, he knew he couldn't just walk away. He had to set things right, even if it meant total rejection.

He turned, took a deep breath, and started forward.

They didn't see him coming, not until he reached out and tapped Renee on the shoulder. "Hey, dudes," he said with a smile. Oops! Wrong intro. Try again. "I mean . . . hi, guys. Mind if I hang with you?"

Renee looked up. It was hard to read what she was thinking. Without a word she turned to Jordan. Jordan hesitated, then turned to Philip. All three looked at each other. It seemed to take forever for them to make up their minds. Finally, in perfect three-part unison, they shook their heads and said,"Nahhhhhhh"—and turned their backs on him.

Nicholas's heart sank. He'd heard of rejection, but this gave the word a whole new meaning. "Guys?" he pleaded to their backs.

They didn't budge. Not for a whole millisecond. Then they couldn't hold it in any longer. They started giggling . . . first a little, then a lot. Finally they turned back to Nicholas, laughing. Renee tousled his hair, Jordan poked his stomach, and Philip gave him a punch on the arm. Nick knew they each, in their own ways, were saying, "We're glad you're back . . . but don't you ever, ever do that to us again!"

He broke into a grin. He wanted to say something powerful, something profound, something that would show the depths of his feelings. But all that came out was a thick kind of "I'm sorry," followed by an embarrassed shrug.

His friends understood perfectly.

"We wondered when you were gonna shrug off those ice cubes," Jordan said with a smirk.

Pointing at his clothes, Renee quipped, "We thought they'd shrink-wrapped your brain in black leather."

"OK, OK," Nick laughed. "All I can do is plead temporary insanity."

Everyone laughed in agreement. This was easier than Nick had imagined. They'd forgiven him almost instantly. But maybe that's one of the main ingredients of "uncoolness" . . . loving enough to forgive.

Suddenly the room exploded in applause! Dad had just ended his number with a big flourish, and the crowd went wild! Dad beamed. Not only did he manage to impress the crowd, he looked a little impressed himself. And then, at last, he caught Nicholas's eye.

But instead of shrinking or ducking his head, Nick actually raised his arm and gave him a thumbs-up. Dad turned and looked behind himself to see who his son was motioning to, but there was no one in back of him. He turned to Nick, giving him the ol' "Who? Me?" gesture.

Nick laughed.

Dad grinned and stepped off the stage. Immediately he was joined by Mom as he moved through the congratulating crowd—but he barely slowed down. He was determined to reach his son.

When his parents finally arrived, Nick struggled for the right words, but nothing came. That was OK; no words were necessary. Somehow Dad already knew. He smiled and gave Nicholas a brief hug—a very brief hug (after all, they were still surrounded by junior highers). But it made no difference to Nick. For the first time in a long while, he didn't care about being embarrassed.

But it wasn't entirely over—not just yet . . .

When the boy blunder and Pops finished their little huggy-huggy scene, I figured it was time to make my reappearance. After all, Nicky boy had definitely learned his lesson. It was time for me to stop giving him the silent treatment and come out of hiding. (The fact that he started to imagine me again didn't hurt, either.)

"You know, kid," I said as I hopped up on his foot, "I kinda missed ya."

He looked down and yelped, "McGee! You're back!"

"Not only my back," I quipped as I turned around, "but also my fabulous front and two sensational sides."

Nick gave me one of his world-famous "McGee-I-love-you-but-knock-it-off-with-the-stupid-jokes" looks.

Quicker than you can say, "It looks like we're

coming to the end of this little tale," I hopped off his shoe and went over to my souped-up, cherry red McGeemobile. Throwing on my goggles and scarf, I crossed over and opened the hood. "It took a while, but I'm glad you finally found out what's cool."

"You're right," Nick agreed. "Being who you are, that's what's really cool."

"No, no, no," I corrected. "It's cars. Cars are what's cool!"

I ducked my head (and everything else except for my toes) under the hood. "Three-eighty-five, dual cams, overdrive—it doesn't get much cooler than this."

"McGee," the kid started to protest.

"Watch this!" I shouted as I slammed down the hood and hopped behind the wheel.

"What are you doing?" Nick asked in obvious jealousy.

"Peelin' rubber," I said with a grin as I stepped on the gas. "WHOOOAAA . . . NELLIE!"

I took off and left a skid mark the size of the national debt on the floor. I never knew such power. I never knew such speed. I never learned how to drive . . .

"L O O K O U T ! ! !"

It was demolition derby time.

VVVAAAROOOOOOOOOOOOOM!

Everywhere I turned there were shoes . . . hundreds of dancing shoes. I swerved back and forth and back and forth. And then, when I got tired of that, I started swerving forth and back and forth and back.

It did no good. I couldn't keep this up forever. It

was time to do what I did best: time to assert my genuinely great genius, to motivate my manly machoness, to scream my head off for help.

"NICHOLAS!"

But that didn't do any good, either. Ol' Nicky was too busy pointing and laughing. And then, finally, it happened. There were no more shoes. Ah, what luck, what fortune, what FEAR!!

"Somebody . . . move that stage!!"

There it was, dead ahead (a rather unfortunate choice of words, but have you ever heard of something being "live ahead?" I didn't think so). In any case, I was heading straight toward the stage. Not a bad place for someone with my great talents, but at the moment I had no more songs or jokes. I'd left all my song-and-dance stuff back in chapter 5.

But not to worry your pretty little heads, dear reader. I'll get out of this. I always do. Besides, Book Twelve is just around the corner, and you wouldn't dream of reading a book with just the title "And Me!" on the cover. Right?

I mean you'd want another name in the front. Right? Something that starts with "Mc" . . . and maybe ends in a couple of "e"s . . . with a big "G" stuck in the middle?

Right?

Ahem, I said, "Right?"

OK. Fine. If you want to be that way about it, you'll just have to excuse me. I have a little more screaming to do.

"NICHOLAS!! GET ME OUT OF HERE! N I C H O-L A S ! ! ! ! !"